Wordsplash Hodgepodge

by

Joanne Faries

Wordsplash Hodgepodge

by
Joanne Faries

Acknowledgements

To Ray

To my family and friends

To all readers

Special thanks to the world of Blogging
A-to-Z and its creators

Wordsplash Hodgepodge
Table of Contents

A to Z Poetry

Hodgepodge Poetry Medley

Hodgepodge - A to Z Poetry

Apropos

of nothing
I write this poem
as I contemplate the alphabet
string together words
silly beats seek a sly smile
from A to Z, we shall wonder
as we wander to a place of

Zen

Bored

you never mentioned boredom in my mother's
presence
she could rustle up a work project before the
words
left your mouth
she would slap a brush or a rag into your hand,
clippers or a
shovel and point in all directions
oh she was slick, and fast, setting a pace
that left you pleading for release from your house
arrest

to this day, I'm never bored. I might be on a
slowdown
or between projects. Antsy and distracted
contemplating life choices
but never bored

or that voice in my head (sounds an awful lot like
mom)
steers me into motion
and something gets

cleaned

Clean

slate for the new year
but smudges remain, traces linger
I trip over baggage
chunked in the spare room
compartmentalized in the brain
nudged into view by a comment,
an email, or even a song
old friends remember
relatives rehash
laughter muffled as you enter
shush exclaimed as you leave
sideways glances, furrowed brow
keep wiping, make amends
face the year
without

d
r
e
a
d

Dread

return from vacation
loose limbed lope
tightens, shoulders hunch
stomach rumble
heartbeat hassle

clock watching witness
time now stands still
folders piled haphazardly
pink urgent notes jumbled
amidst post-it-note reminders

meetings scheduled, teleconference
turmoil, gossip train rolls over
relaxation memory
stiff collar irritates fading sunburn
soul trapped until next vacation

elation

Elation

is more than overall happiness
it's the sheer delight,
absolute joy of a moment
it's reaching the top of the rollercoaster
spotting a soaring eagle
being swept up by a crowd cheer
anticipating the moment your taxi
zooms out of the tunnel and you are overwhelmed
surrounded by skyscrapers and humanity

elation is a welcome hug at baggage claim
familiar face aglow with love

never

forgotten

Forget

I wrote forgotten before
dismiss this omission
disregard the lack of effort
maybe I seek oblivion
but no matter how hard I try
I can't forget

no, I won't forget

you

I grapple with the ghost

Grapple

with life struggles
pshaw, the world snorts
at my innocence
grasp the concept of despair
desperation, naïve I give to charity
feel like I made a difference
while people clutch at air
shuffle their tarot cards
too much death, no gold

pray for heaven as they live a hell

Heaven

heavens to betsy, this poetry has gotten
far too serious. Now hell would be serious, warm
and toasty
but probably not fun like heaven
so let's go light or lite and think about rainbows,
chocolate, seeing folks we miss (my Mom, my
Nana),
and being young and thin and carefree again
or still old and pudgy but carefree again
throw away the glasses, no aches or pains
green grass, blue skies, and fields of flowers
beaches, and butterflies, mountains, and fountains
heaps of mashed potatoes, and endless enchiladas
whimsical roundtables with endless laughs
soaring music with choirs of rock angels
peace and love and peace and love
and peace and love and peace and love

heaven should be peace and love to

infinity

Infinity

that's my love for Ray
he deserves a shout out in a poem
puts up with so much crap
artsty need to putz
create and bizarre humor
twenty something years of marriage
he's carried my crap
with a smile
and well, maybe I've done my share too
we are together for infinity

life is

joyous, jubilant, and juicy

Juicy

grapefruit ruby red
slurp jump starts the day with a tang
multi-napkin breakfast

oh, you were expecting juicy gossip?
I'll never tell, I jabber in jest
my real life bores on paper
muddle along, stay out of the way
of trauma, drama, and jargon

oh I can kvetch, kibitz, and throw
kindling on the bonfire of conjecture
or smile and wink on the subject of kink

seriously...it was just a

kiss

Kiss

so keen, moment keepsake
keystone of our essence
kickoff to our karma

kismet

knitted, kneaded, and knotted
knowledge leads to our

life and love

labryrinth

Labyrinth

layers of levity
liberal doses of labor
languish in languages of love

easy to be lackadaisical
easier to lapse
marriage license to laziness

unacceptable

no limits to listen
and learn and look
and explore the labyrinth

of love's

madcap marvelous

melody

Melody

memorable tunes conjure magic
maze – years of journey
made mystical or mushy

Motown beat
ball of confusion
stopped us in the name of love
all there in a toe tapping moment

myriad years of soul, rock, pop
newfangled disco or grunge
set the mood

 for now or

negligee or

never

Never

nuzzle a porcupine

sidle up with care
nuggets of wisdom
not appreciated
notice the mood,
numb to nosegays or nuance
don't be a nuisance
numskulls nudge rather
than nurture

observe obstacles

Obstacles

obliterate dreams
obvious traps occur

overrule offbeat operations
opt for opportunity
remain optimistic no matter
the ordeal

too easy to oscillate
overwhelmed

preparation, perspiration
overcome

paralysis

Paralyzed

panicked deadline passed
blank page paranoia
writers' curse
peel plot onionskin to reveal
puff pastry, piffle

penchant for dismal prose
perpetrate pretty poetry

pronounced a

quack

Quack

writer quandary
question quality

quietly quenching a thirst
sharpen the quill and query

characters quarrel
wander to the quay
final quip

your day job…

don't quit

seek another

raison d'etre

Raison d'etre

justification for living
sounds fancier in French
urgent and compelling

rationale for the rat race
realistic razzle-dazzle

the more I read, the less I know
rave or resign
revelation or revolution

still seek a reason and
succumb to the sojourn

Sojourn

soldier on he says
solemn in his faith
her soul is struck by Neil Diamond's
Song Sung Blues
they separate

she staggers, he stomps
stalemate
synchronicity simplicity
she salivates for his love
he seeks salvation

both quench a

thirst

Thirst

for knowledge, yearn for enlightenment
quench the spirit and soul
slake the dry parched throat
then cram words into the brain

quite the

undertaking

Undertake

to understand the human condition
I always feel like the understudy in my life
caught in the undertow
in my underwear

certainly undermined by doubts
universal need to unlock key to utopia

I vacillate

Vacillate

valiant effort to vacate
my negativity
vague yearnings in vain
to remove the villain in my life – me
I need a vision or a vacation
vital desire to

win or

waffle

Waffle

I prefer blueberry or maybe one with strawberries
and cream

You expected me to wade into a bigger issue?
War, waste, welfare?
Nah, let's whistle or whittle

waft on a breeze into the wild and
ask why?

Why not eat a waffle for dinner – maybe smother it
in honey and pecans?

Why write this poem?

to make my mark in this world
my

X

make a mark and move on

yonder

Yonder

hop aboard your yacht or a yak
take a year
spin a yarn
tales of yore
reflect on yesterday
yodel or yell
with

zeal

Zeal

I am a zombie by now in my zest
to zoom through letter poems
zany ride to the

zenith

we zipped along together
zigzag

alphabet zoo

thanks for joining me
from

A to Z

Hodgepodge – Poetry Medley

Adrift At Sea

no more landline

I can't reach to the wall to hear
another political message
no one can offer me pest control
or carpet cleaning

last vestige of a clear signal

gone

now a conversation will be filled with
huh? What? Repeat that please

progress in a tiny handheld device
but I can send you a picture too

I remember rotary

wireless? That's crazy talk

now hands free in a car
words rise to a cloud

but as I think about it
I really have nothing to say

Sprinkler Dash

walked the neighborhood the other day
said hello to a young man
he moved a hand sprinkler around his yard
as I watched the water flow

back and forth

        back and forth

                back and forth

I yearned to put on my swim suit and dash through
the spray

oh such a treat when mom conceded to our pleas
my brother and I had such a splendid time
leaps, bounds, cartwheels, and silly dances
giggles rippled as the water cooled

our bare feet, arms, and legs

now I stand and watch a young man move a hand
sprinkler
around a front yard, no kids in sight

except this big kid who took off her sandal
stuck her foot into the spray
and giggled

Measles at Age Four

red spots exploded
every inch speckled
fevered dreams
drenched in weariness
mom offered ginger ale
bendy straw for cracked lips
curtains shuttered
avoid sun weakened eyes
head ached, throat scratched
no interest in cartoons
signaled fever spiral

emerge from haze
limp, hard fought battle won
perhaps future kids
can avoid this disease

Whir

garage door opens
signals arrival of my love
he tosses keys, frowns, cycles mail
slowly shakes off the work day
hangs dress trousers
crumpled shirt thrown
into laundry bin
dons jeans and t-shirt
he can breathe
laces sneakers and smiles
"walk around the block?"

Airline Counter Woes

expectations and brochures
pour over maps
trace paths of imagination
inhale a memory
exhale a moment
fumble for luggage
one piece chose a different flight

lines and lines and lines
to claim loss

inner scream like the two year old who is

S C R E A M I N G

yellow splash

amidst crunchy brown grass
flower stalks bent after
january freeze
shed shriveled leaves
forlorn garden remnants
gasp, surprised by tepid days
shocked by bitter cold nights
wind chill factor fury

yellow burst blazes
blisters raw winter canvas

one dandelion

smile

feather flake wisps

swirl outside my window
layers of gray clouds
explode like a pillow fight
dervish whirlwind of white
blankets the earth
shroud of calm
muffled sounds
until boot crunch steps
erase the pristine land

Missed His Turn

informal line at the swings
kids hovered, willed the pig-tailed girl to finish
boy in torn tee swung higher and higher
narrowly missed oblivious pre-teen texting
brothers pushed each other, swapped turns
hogged the far left, ignored pleas to share
lean girl, long hair streamed behind her
dangled her feet and twirled slowly
dizzy, she relinquished her swing
staggered to the jungle gym
eight year old in blue jeans
hesitated, one step too slow
heavyset boy elbowed him
plopped and pushed off
to open mouthed shock
brazen line breaker
sneered

Mt. Vesuvius Looms

uncovered from layers of ashes
Pompeii's energetic
ancient life appeared
grindstones for bread
foyers and courtyards
government buildings
gladiator training centers
lavish spas and stone bed brothels

I bent to touch embedded mosaic
ran my finger across a chariot groove
admired painted frescos
basked in the amphitheater's warmth
contemplated AD 79, rumbled warnings
unparalleled disaster ahead
for folks with oil lamps seeking
shelter, as marble stones reflected a safe path home

Vesuvius spewed deadly gasses
invaded lungs and conquered a seaport
enveloped a society
it hovers today
harmless green mountain
bides its time
history on its side
silent sinister death

No Wriggle Room

you must sit still
Mama gives her look
wiggled toes in shoes
dodgy evasion by the book

blink your eyes a lot
do not shake your head
clench your fists one at a time
remember what Mama said

ice cream treat awaits
if butt stays in chair
no swinging legs
oh, she stays aware

avoid stuck out tongue
twists, crunches, or kicks
take deep belly breaths
watch the clock ticks

contemplate yummy choices
vanilla swirl or chocolate chip
attacked by nose itch
imagine first bite, lick your lip

bow head, say amen
Mama nods and smiles
ooze off bench, jitterbug
time to run in place for miles

All Sides of Life

white haired and stooped
silver haired and slowing
two men breakfasted every Thursday
corn beef hash and wheat toast
pancakes and bacon
one coffee, one orange juice

smiles on the side

regular place, regular booth, regular chat
neighbors
originals to the neighborhood
catty-corner back lawn
past the one with the added hedge
no fences

history on their side

kids, church, couples bridge
dinners, New Year's, and Halloween
until the women passed
one sudden heart attack
one lingering cancer
widowers now retired

no one by their side

breakfast tradition began
only missed by vacation
an illness, snowstorm or two
years rolled by, friendship grew

common ground trod
eggs or French toast variation

biscuits on the side

one met a lady friend
moved to senior home
the other stayed with his roots
Thursday breakfast remained
tradition upheld
until the call came

farewell from bedside

my dad's good buddy
gone now, sad to say
fifty-five years of friendship
hard to fathom these days
no more breakfast tickets
hearty laughs or retread tales

stay at home on Thursdays now

stay inside

And Then There Was One

I hate being precious
stuck in a stroller
dandy outfit complete with hat
matching striped socks, and new red shoes
I hate shoes, but they are a challenge
must begin my campaign with a winner
new parent, rookie mistakes. I have lung power
advantage
wail and head shake. Arm flaps.
hand slaps hat askew
red faced I sniffle.

Mom straightens hat, but I renew effort
another arm wave whoosh, unencumbered head
Dad surrenders, picks up hat, stuffs it in bag
I giggle, gurgle, drool so Mom bends down to wipe
my mouth and kiss my forehead. She smiles

oh this is too easy

we roll along a path in fits and bursts. Camera
shots
parents babble, distracted by sights
I wriggle my toes scrunched in these shoes
concentrate on right one
rub against foot rest, it loosens
I jabber, bounce in my seat with glee
kick and catch an edge
right shoe sails on to sidewalk close to grass

one happy foot

jailbreak joy

Freedom

chubby legs churned pedals
unaware of parental release
forward focus, no looking back
giddy grin, breeze ruffled hair
uneven training wheels
high pitched clatter
she rode confident
until German shepherds barked
strained leashes tied to a neighbor tree
distracted, head turned, sought reassurance
saw guiding hand a block away
she wavered

unsteady cyclist
veered left into curb
slow motion spill
wheels spun slowly as she untangled
tear trickle sob, scraped knee
accepted parent hug
she hobbled alongside
righted bike, dad steered
stopped. "Hop back on."
tear stained face grimaced
he nodded, she hesitated
eased onto seat, slow pedal home

don't let go, daddy

I have to, sweetheart

Sounds of Italy

gladiator echo in the Colosseum
ruts of chariot wheels in Pompeii
ancient rumble of carts hauling wares
operatic arias reverberate in Venice
gondolier chatter, tourist camera clicks
shopkeeper patter, rustle of money exchange
Latin chant rolls with the mists surrounding Assisi
slurp of gelato tongue tingle
shoe shuffle stumble on cobblestones
inner grazie for the life concerto

Hodgepodge Flash

Peace and Quiet

As one of the first Peace Corps volunteers, I had
no idea what I was doing. 1961, Linda, Tom, and I
emerged from a prop plane in the Congo, climbed
into an ancient Jeep, and rattled over non-existent
roads to a jungle shantytown. Our mission as
engineering graduates - water drainage, malaria
education, and peace.

Unearthly keening outside our huts kept us wide-
eyed that first night. Linda greeted the morning
with a curse as she stepped outside, "Ouch, damn.
Molly, Come here." She'd stumbled over a
makeshift shrine - odd carvings, bones, and
feathers cluttered the doorway. Tom's entrance was
also blocked.

Our ominous beginning continued. No one joined
us at the well. "Town is empty," said Tom after a
brief drive. "Doors ajar, carts overturned. It's
eerie."

"Should we leave?" I asked. Tom shrugged, pulled
out pre-approved plans, and grabbed a shovel.

"If I go back, I have to get a real job," he said.

We worked steadily and made progress despite
exhaustion. Night wailing continued. No sign of
the source. We sweltered. Two weeks in, I awoke
to find Linda slipping out the door. "Have to stop

that noise. I'll be back." As I got up to follow her, the high-pitched screams stopped. But Linda didn't return.

Frantic, I banged on Tom's door. No answer, so I barged in. No Tom. Only a note on his bed - don't look under the floorboards. I staggered to the Jeep, hesitated, peeked.

Can't stop shrieking.

Wrestle With Love

Ari and Elizabeth pushed and pulled furniture into place in their small London flat. She settled into her rocking chair. "Oh Ari, we can watch telly, and still visit with friends. It's cozy."

"Cozy means my bean bag chair is gone."

"Cozy means we're grownups, not flopped on the floor like university. Stop pouting and give me a kiss," Elizabeth puckered. Ari groused and gave her a proper buss.

"You want me to be straight with you, right?" Ari asked. "All candour?" She frowned but nodded. "This has to go." He pointed at her macramé wall hanging.

"Seriously?"

He gave the outta here sign. She contemplated the art, arose, reluctantly removed it, and asked, "What now, Ari? No sports posters."

"No, I want our wedding picture there. I love you."

"I love you, too. But I need more time."

He stayed silent, and she returned to her rocker. "My family in Dublin ..."

"… need to meet me." He finished her sentence. "Then it will all be fine?" His dark eyebrows narrowed and his brown eyes gleamed. She leaned to run her fingers through his long dark curls.

"Oh Ari. It's not like I say rosary every day, but conversion to Judaism … it's huge."

He flicked on the television. Shocked, the two cried as announcers pronounced, "They're all gone. Israeli athletes murdered at these 1972 Munich Olympics."

Elizabeth whispered, "All candour, Ari. I love you too much. Yes." She stopped from crossing herself. "I will marry you."

Published in *Doorknobs & Bodypaint* 69, February 2013

Classical Career

My resume shone as an example of striving for
perfection and appearing to falling short. I stood in
a warehouse before a table. Taxis honked outside.
The aroma of Chinese food wafted in the air. A
man and woman suppressed snickers as they
reviewed my life, as printed on fine linen paper.

It was 1981. I graduated cum laude with a degree
from Valley City State University, North Dakota.
Mining? Norwegian as a Second Language? Nope.
Classical music. Instrument - the harp.

The redheaded woman looked up. "What are you
doing here? How did the screener let you
through?"

I smiled and said, "Avoiding welfare. I need a job. I
know music, and the screener is a New York
second cousin twice removed. We Larssons stick
together."

She frowned and asked the bearded dude,
"Screener's name?"

"Lisa Larsson."

"Lucky break, kid. What do you know about music
videos?"

I shrugged. "Not much, but I can write about
intricacies of lyrics, layers of percussion, and fill

dead air. I assume Music Video Television avoids silence. Lisa told me. Like radio d-jays, your v-jays have to maintain flow, persuade viewers to watch the next video."

She held up my resume. "Creative cover letter."

"Try me for a week. MTV V-jays will ooze dulcet tones, exude backbeats of patter, and teach kids a whole new language. Gossip and hair metal."

They both nodded. "One week trial." He paused, "You really majored in harp?"

"Yep, with a tambourine, music theory, and typing back-up plan."

Published in *Doorknobs & Bodypaint* 70, May 2013

Something Stinks

Tom Cordona put the Cadillac in drive, wiped the steering wheel, then with a flourish placed the handkerchief neatly in his breast pocket. He stepped out of the car. I watched from the passenger seat, still strapped in, blood seeped from a bullet hole in my side. My eyes flickered, yearned to close, but I wouldn't give him that satisfaction. I struggled to sit up, maintain composure, and glare at him.

"Stella, you're a feisty one, but you got in too deep, sweetheart. Why did you come to the docks and open that door?"

"I figured you were two-timing me, Tom. I only followed you from the restaurant because I was sick of Chanel. As if I didn't smell it on your clothes?" I exhaled and pressed my hand to my side. The blood oozed, and my body ached.

He replied, sounded far away. I turned my head to see that he still stood at the car door, not touching anything, a slight frown on his face. "I never cheated on you, Stella. You classed me up - just look at you with that chestnut hair, va-va-voom body, and an education. I mean, half the time I had no idea what you were telling me, but it sounded so swell. All the guys were impressed, but they warned me." He waggled a finger at me. "Smart dames are trouble, Tommy."

At this I closed my eyes, giving in to the pain of his words and the gunshot. After a pause, I said, "So the Chanel was a cover for the fancy French wines you hustled. No laws on perfume, but the feds discouraged booze."

"Yeah, and you working for the mayor ... how'd that look? You had to nose around." Tom shrugged. "This ...this is business. Dominick said you gotta disappear."

Dark spots before my eyes and lightheadedness didn't bode well. I coughed and the metallic taste increased my nausea. My resolve to not cry wavered.

One final gamble. I had to keep my pride. No begging, no wailing. I whispered, "Tom, if I'm not at work tomorrow, the mayor will come after you. There's a letter in my desk drawer - gives him your name, address, Dom's info."

"You're bluffing, Stella," he said with bravado. Yet his eyelids fluttered. Betrayed doubt. I knew his tell and I had him questioning himself. He got back in the Cadillac and fired her up. "You got a key to your office?"

I nodded. Blood pooled at my feet. I was dying, but not headed into the ocean. I willed myself to hang on, for the satisfaction of pulling a gun from my office drawer - my farewell letter to Tom.

Window Dressed Love

Angelina applied makeup. She glanced in the mirror for final approval and was pleased with her tawny tresses' cooperation. Her rose negligee clung in appropriate places. She was ready to face Trace, the premier male window dressing model. She'd prayed for this assignment.

The goal today was to entice tourists to stop, stare, and choose to enter the store. The bonus goal was to appear on Trace's radar. But first they had to mesmerize, create an illusion of domesticity heated by G-rated sex. After all, they were on THE premier New York City Avenue and represented THE premier shopping experience.

"Hey," Trace said as he entered the window. "Are you sitting or standing first?"

"Um, stand at the stove and pose?" she asked. Then she declared, "I'll stand. I'm making you breakfast." She exhaled.

"Great. I'll read the paper. At the twenty minute mark, kiss me as you serve pancakes or whatever."

Her heart fluttered at the thought of brushing her lips against his.

"Yo, you okay?" asked Trace. "You look flushed. Flu's going around. I don't want to catch nothin'. If you're sick, call in another model."

"No, no. It's all good," she reassured him. "So, you ready for the holidays?" She decided to warm him up with chitchat.

"Nah, not really into Christmas. I'm psyched for New Year's. Flying to Gstaad to ski. That's the only place to be these days. "

"Cool," Angelina said. *How can I keep up? Holy crap. He's a golden god, heading to freakin' Switzerland.*

Trace glanced at his watch. "And we are on the clock. Minimal movement. Get your pose comfortable. I'll give a count in fifteen."

She angled herself toward the window, spatula in hand at the stove. Tourists and Trace could admire her full breasts and long legs.

Fifteen minutes segments flew by as they posed, moved. At one point, Angelina sat on Trace's lap and could feel the stir of his privates. Tourists peered into the windows and inspired by hot domestic bliss were inspired to buy placemats, cookware, and loungewear. Little did they know that the pancake-serving kiss initiated an invite to ski.

Unfortunately Trace had not brushed his teeth that morning. Angelina's desire for passion resulted in derision. *OMG, the sexiest model in NYC is a pig.*

Bourbon and cigarettes. She gulped air once free from his embrace.

The final fifteen minutes were torturous. Trace moved into position behind her. People from Iowa and God knows where watched Trace fan his fingers down her arm. A girl outside screamed.

"So," Trace murmured in her ear. "Gstaad? We'd look great on the slopes together."

Angelina shook her head. "Nope, Georgia. Slop Granny Gertrude's pigs. "

Published in *Doorknobs & Bodypaint*, 69, February 2013

Snow Plowed

It takes a lot of snow to stop life in Maine, but Trevor and I were holed up at the Bangor Motel. Separate rooms, of course. We were here on forestry business - a symposium. However, the keynote speaker had pneumonia, flights were cancelled, and only a few hardy souls drove in from respective parks. Muffled chains churned through snowpack, and my four-wheel-drive Jeep rarely slipped. Concentrating on the road was tedious, and I was wired.

I got up and knocked on Trevor's door. "One second," he said, before opening it. "Can't rest, Rita? Me, neither. Think there's a bar here?" I nodded and he slipped his room card into his pocket and shut the door. "What the heck, it's a snow day, right?"

We padded down the hallway, the swirl patterned carpet hiding years of use. We worked in two different state parks, but communicated through the year. Graduates of University of Maine, Trevor and I had been in the same orbit for ten years.

Settled at the bar with a local brew, we tapped mugs and had a swig. "So Rita, what's new in your neck of the woods?" He rolled his long-lashed green eyes at the oldest forestry joke in history. I inwardly swooned, my old school girl crush refused to die.

We chatted about our parks and environment issues. "I'd ban snowmobiles," he said. "Hate those suckers."

"Cross country skiing is my favorite way to patrol. The swoosh of the skis, the slight ting from the poles, exhaled misty breath, and the sun glint from the snow," I waxed poetic, infused with beer, camaraderie, and mutual park love.

Trevor's ruddy cheeks vouched for his time outdoors. "That's profound. Let's go ski. Now."

"Now?"

"Sure, snowstorm's let up. There are woods behind us. Got your gear?"

"Well, yeah."

"C'mon." We hustled to our rooms to change. Emerging at the same time, we walked out the lobby door, and strapped on our skis. I raised my face, stuck out my tongue, and caught a snowflake. Trevor mimicked me, then stuck in his poles and took off. I scrambled to follow. We skied for thirty minutes, and stopped to rest on a fallen log.

"You know, Rita, you're my kind of gal. Ski at a moments notice. No fuss. Just slap on a woolen hat and go," said Trevor. "We've known each other a long time."

Where was this going? He hugged me.

Trevor turned and kissed my cheek. "I'm going to miss you." He paused, " ... and this." He raised a ski pole to the woods. "Hawaii, Rita. I got the Maui assignment."

I inhaled Bangor's cold air and exhaled. "Aloha, Trevor. Aloha."

Published in *Doorknobs & Bodypaint*, 69 February 2013

Hodgepodge Additional Chapters:
The Tale Goes On

She's Gone Batty

My Zoo World brought you my adventures with creatures great and small. I don't hate animals. I'm just leery of their intentions. Hence, my fear and hesitation as I walk in this wild kingdom called earth. As I discovered, my published book said The End, but there is more to the tale.

It was an innocent spring day in Texas. Blue sky, fresh breeze. Perfect for a patio sit and read after a long day at work. Ever mindful of the sun, I cranked the umbrella and sat down with a magazine.

Movement. I sensed movement out of the corner of my eye. I raised my head and near the top of the umbrella, something black rustled. What was it? I scooted closer to take a look. As I did, the small creature opened to reveal a small pink mouth bearing teeth. As it hissed, I shrieked and leaped back.

What a hullaballoo! It flapped its webbed wings and careened about the umbrella. I flapped my arms as I gathered my reading material, phone, and drink. I don't think my feet touched the ground.

I scurried into the house, ducking and weaving. Slam. Door shut, lock engaged. I breathed deeply and dialed Ray. "I was attacked by a bat."

"What are you talking about?" Ray used his calm voice.

"Umbrella up…hissed….vampire teeth….wings flapping. We scared each other." Indeed, I recognized that I disturbed a perfectly good bat nap. I'm sure he was cozy snoozing in the material folds. But he was on my territory.

"Did he fly away?"

"No, he followed me toward the house, swooping. I think he went behind the outdoor picture on the wall."

Ray sighed. "He'll be fine there. I'm almost home. I'm sure he just wanted darkness. He's hunkered down for now."

"Hurry," I begged.

I peered out the patio door. No sign of movement. I unlocked and stepped outside. Quiet. Not a creature stirring. I gathered my stuff and proceeded to settle in under the umbrella. Nervous, I read but scanned the area constantly. Alert and ready to evacuate at any hint of winged attack.

Tap, tap. I startled. Ray was home and grinning as he tapped the window. He knew I'd leap. Glad to accommodate.

Changed out of work clothes, Ray stepped outside and asked, "Okay, where's Batman?"

I pointed to the flip-flop picture." I'm sure he flew to the wall and scooted behind our art." Ray grabbed a broom and inched closer to the hanging object. He lifted one end and I squealed.

"Shush. I see him. It's tiny." He looked at me and rolled his eyes. "He's fine right there."

Wrong thing to say. "No, he needs to leave our environs. Fly to the field or something. Go catch bugs."

"Okay. Go inside. I'll take care of this." I oozed inside, nose pressed to the window.

Ray flung the picture off the wall and used the broom to nudge the bat. He was already flapping, disturbed once again. Fortunately, he chose to evacuate the patio. With one final swoop, he did a barrel roll and flew out of sight.

Mission accomplished. Ray was my hero once again. No bats in this belfry or umbrella. I can stop wearing garlic around my neck.

Bob & Weave

Trish and I chattered away as we rounded a curve
at River Legacy Park. It was a warm but overcast
Friday in Texas. Both off work, we met for lunch
at La Madeleine and an agreed upon walk in the
park. Unlike weekends with bikers, roller skaters,
and families galore, the park was quiet, almost
hushed.

We both stopped dead in our tracks and said,
"Whoa."

Strolling out from the grasses was a bobcat. He was
nonchalant, and had his back to us. No doubt he
knew we were there, but not concerned. A beam of
sunlight shone through dappled leaves, bearing
witness to his tawny splendor. I say he, not
knowing anything about size or gender indications.
He was alone.

"I've seen bobcats before out here," whispered
Trish. "Not uncommon. We'll be fine."

I was a tad nervous, after all this was a very fast
creature with claws and teeth. Trish ran for fun and
fitness. I did not. I could be caught easily.
However, common sense said the bobcat had a
different mission in mind.

Sure enough, he bounded back into the grassy
woodlands. A graceful leap. We paused and did not

hear anything else. With a mutual nod, we resumed our walk, tentative and aware.

As we neared where the bobcat had been, we slowed and gave a wide berth left of the path and then stopped. Hunkered down, *Bob* did not twitch. He was intent on his prey, concentrating. A slight swish in the grasses, some poor creature attempting to flee had no idea what fate loomed.

Trish and I held our breath and watched. Not a flicker. Then whoosh! A massive pounce, lots of rustling, and then quiet. Poof, the bobcat was gone, no doubt enjoying his lunch entrée or perhaps dessert.

That's a lot of nature to witness. Impressive and scary too. We walked in the nature preserve, bob and weaved along a path of death. We lived with nary a scratch.

The only shot I took was a picture on my phone. Yes, there's proof and it's not blurry from shaking.

Seriously, a Toe?

In **Athletic Antics,** I brought you humorous tales of misfortune and calamity in the world of sport, skill, and coordination. Here's a new tale of woe concerning a toe. Seriously?

Summer 2015, typical Texas heat. Minimal clothes required. Often wore flip-flops but for a quick jaunt out front to get the mail, I was barefoot. Got the mail, and then sidetracked to pluck a weed. Hot pavement. Moved too quickly (for me). Jammed my foot on an edger pavestone.

Ouch! That hurt. It's going to leave a mark. My toes were scraped a bit, but no blood. No foul. Onward inside, unaware of the trauma I wrought with my dexterity and grace.

A week or so later, a toe twinge. No bruising, no obvious damage, but depending on shoes or certain movement, my second toe on the right foot said, "Hey, what are you doing?"

I shrugged, shook it off as tender, and went about my business. Walking, swimming. All good.
Or not. More pain and a need to limp. Time to see my podiatrist.

Dr. Jeff Taylor delivered the news after X-rays and tenderly yanking on my toe enough to make me jump. "Torn tendon. This will not heal on its own and requires surgery."

"What? It's just a toe."

"Yes, a toe that needs to be attached to the foot."

I scheduled surgery for end of September. A multitude of things happened that caused me to postpone the surgery. I could walk. It was fine. I needed to get back east and help my siblings with my father. He needed care. My toe could wait.

Oh, for such a teeny thing, my toe squawked. It reminded me it was still hanging on …barely.…

New Year, new insurance, new mess. That's another book. The February surgery was canceled. Another insurance shuffle occurred and finally April rolled around and I rolled into the operating room.

By this time, my toe had decided to secede from my foot. It was quite detached and required some extra love and care and metal work. I awoke with a boot on my foot and instructions to stay off it for two weeks. Ice and elevation were my mantra.

Two more weeks on crutches with the boot and no driving. This healing "sport" injury stuff was annoying and tiresome. I had a lot of respect now for athletes who come back from surgery better, faster, and stronger.

I followed instructions and truly my toe chose to align and heal fairly quickly. I behaved – no dancing, hiking, or marathons.

Not that a marathon was ever on my bucket list, but it would be tricky to do even as I approached the one year mark. Walking just wasn't my strong suit.

So, I've told the truth, but as time has worn on, I've got a better story. I hurt the toe as a stunt double for Black Widow in the *Avenger* movie. The toe was sacrificed for the sake of the shot. Hey, it could have happened.

Stop snickering.

Seriously, for the sake of my toe, stop chortling.

End

About the author

Joanne Faries, originally from the Philadelphia area, lives in Texas with her husband Ray. She graduated from Temple University (BBA) and University of Texas Arlington (MBA), but she should have pursued liberal arts. After years in office management, she was fortunate to leave the world of electronics and pursue her writing dream. A part-time job as a documentation specialist for Omega Research keeps her in pen and paper. Published in *Doorknobs & Bodypaint*, and *Chicken Soup for the Soul* books, she also has poems in *Silver Boomer anthologies*. Joanne is the film critic for the *Little Paper of San Saba*. (a town without a cinema).

Look for her humorous memoir *My Zoo World: If All Dogs Go to Heaven, Then I'm in Trouble*, and collection *Wordsplash Flash*, plus the *Wordsplash Poetry Puddle* series. *Athletic Antics* is her latest memoir. All can be found on Amazon

www.wordsplash-joannefaries.blogspot.com

My Zoo World (If All Dogs Go to Heaven, Then I'm in Trouble)

by Joanne Faries

As an animal fearing woman, Joanne Faries laughs at her acclimation to an animal loving world. She stares down swans in Sweden and a guinea pig in the washroom, but averts her eyes for the wombat in Australia.

My Zoo World is a humorous memoir of animal encounters with a twist. Among published animal tales, very few are skewed with a touch of fear and laughter on every page. Unlike books written by pet-loving authors, these chapters introduce the reader to a manic menagerie of animals: a snapping Shetland pony, a bowling ball playing pit bull, and a terrified turtle that tolerates distress. Meet Benji, the cat, Muff, the dog, and more. Friends are convinced they can overcome Joanne's concerns with their precious pets. Join them and root for the animals as you read **My Zoo World.**

Wordsplash Flash by Joanne Faries

Flash Fiction - Tell a story in less than five hundred words. Capture love, hate, and heat on a page. Enhance characters with dialogue or a sigh. Let them bemoan their fate or choose to persevere.

Wordsplash Flash is a collection of sixty stories, none over five hundred words. The book contains four sections: Love/Hate/Love, Saints & Sins, Labor, and Heat. Lose yourself in a corn maze (Maize), stomp on love (Wrath of Grape), and spit watermelon seeds (Toothless Grin). Meet an underwear model (Brief Encounter) or slog in a factory (Press On).

In our hurry-up environment, you need a break. Take a minute to step out of your world and into the past (1940 Theater) or the future (Too Hot to Cold).

Wordsplash Flash tales offer a respite, a laugh, or what just happened? moments.

I hate poetry. I don't understand poetry.
Does this sound familiar?

The **Wordsplash Poetry Puddle: Nature**
collection has no hidden agenda. Words are used to
paint a picture - splash an image on the page.
Words give a sense of calm or transport the reader
to another time. Hear the ocean, feel raindrops,
and immerse oneself in nature.

Little stories are told on each page. Dance in the
puddles with the author.

Sidewalk chalks

smeared rainbow
uneven hopscotch
smudged hearts
crooked flowers
smattering lines

mimic brain waves
of young artist

kid loose on the world
makes a mark
only to hear thunder
rain drops splatter

ephemeral dreams

The **Wordsplash Poetry Puddle: Hazy Memory**
collection reflects on summer joys, baseball, beach
trips, grandmothers, teen years, family, and love.

she joins the YMCA
because she is afraid to fly
her dreams reveal no explosion
yet the plane is dismembered

she, alone

holds the seat cushion
flotation device
and treads water

Wordsplash Poetry Puddle: Tread Water taps
into emotions and taps the typewriter. Some poems
explore fears, dreams, and wayward paths. Other
poems seek shelter in words. Dive into this
collection, and then keep your head above water.

She stood, frozen, at the edge of the diving board. At an early age, Joanne Faries demonstrated absolutely no athletic ability. In **Athletic Antics**, her latest humorous memoir, the author describes riding her bicycle into the back of a car; climbing trees and sliding (not on purpose) down them scraping every inch of her body; plus surviving the duress of junior high field hockey, lacrosse, and volleyball.

YMCA swim achievements (Tadpole, Minnow, Fish, etc.) were halted by the diving board and the teacher nemesis, Ruthie. Would Joanne move on to accomplish Flying Fish and Shark? Could she squint enough to see the other end of the pool?

There are men who sing hallelujah upon the birth of a left-handed son, a future Hall of Fame pitcher. Left-handedness can be a blessing or curse. In archery class, being left-handed did not result in a murder, but it came close. In regards to tennis, Joanne's initial serves baffled her opponents and nabbed a few wins.

Joanne used every English teacher pass excuse possible to work on school newspapers or yearbook, but sooner or later she faced the horror of gymnastics and had to inch her way across the four inch by sixteen-foot balance beam of death. Track and field was not her forte, nor was basketball, soccer, or any sport involving one's hands and/or feet.

As a follow up to her memoir *My Zoo World* about her fear of animals in an animal loving world, Joanne Faries looks at her athletic life in quirky fashion. Laugh at her foibles, identify with her unattractive gym class attire, and fall off the ski tow rope (on the wrong side) with her. *Athletic Antics* covers an assortment of sports, and according to her Wii Fit Plus, Joanne Faries cannot walk a straight line.